DOG BISCUIT

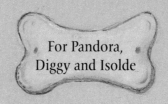

For Pandora,
Diggy and Isolde

DOG BISCUIT   A DOUBLEDAY BOOK
978 0 385 60930 2   Published in Great Britain by
Doubleday, an imprint of Random House
Children's Books   A Random House Group
Company   This edition published   2008
1 3 5 7 9 10 8 6 4 2   Copyright © Helen Cooper, 2008
The right of Helen Cooper to be identified as the
author and illustrator of this work has been
asserted in accordance with the Copyright, Designs
and Patents Act 1988.   All rights reserved.
RANDOM HOUSE CHILDREN'S BOOKS
61–63 Uxbridge Road, London W5 5SA
w w w . **k i d s** a t **r a n d o m h o u s e** . c o . u k
www.rbooks.co.uk   Addresses for companies
within The Random House Group Limited can be
found at: www.randomhouse.co.uk/offices.htm
THE RANDOM HOUSE GROUP Limited Reg. No.
954009   A CIP catalogue record for this book
is available from the British Library.
Printed in Singapore

DOG BISCUIT

Helen Cooper

DOUBLEDAY

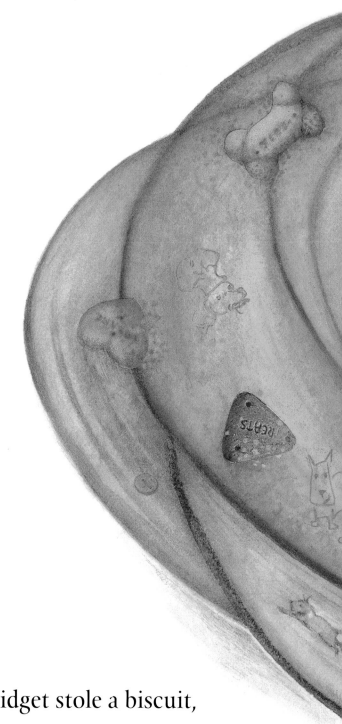

Hungry Bridget stole a biscuit,
found the biscuits in the shed.
They were made for dogs to eat.

But Bridget . . . ate the Dog Biscuit.

IT TASTED SALTY AND SWEET AT THE SAME TIME!

IT TASTED GOOD.

Foolish child!

Mrs Blair found Bridget there
with tell-tale crumbs around her mouth.
"Oh my," she said, and shook her head,
"you'll go bow-wow and turn into a dog."
"Don't tell my mum," begged Bridget.
She wished she hadn't eaten that biscuit.

"I won't say a word," said Mrs Blair and winked.

Mrs Blair's dog winked too.

And Bridget thought she heard it say,

Bridget's mum was rather late.
While they waited, Bridget felt
an itch behind her ears.
Maybe they were growing!

Mum didn't notice a thing.
Bridget wasn't telling.
Mrs Blair waved goodbye,
the dog wagged its tail,
and Bridget wagged her
new tail in reply.

On the way home

they nipped to the Butcher's shop.

Bridget sniffed the air, and tried a few little 'woofs'.

The Butcher smiled at Bridget's mum.
"Good little pup you've got there," he said.
That proved it, didn't it?
Bridget wished she hadn't eaten that biscuit.

Mum still didn't notice a thing.
Bridget wasn't telling.
But at tea time she gobbled her sausage,
and gnawed her chop,

and spilled her milk,

and her brother joined in,

until Dad yelled,

"It's like EATING with a PACK of DOGS!"

At bath time Bridget was a wild dog.

At bed time even wilder.

At story time so full of mischief Dad gave up.

Yet Mum still didn't notice a thing.

Bridget wasn't telling.

Though she wished,

as she curled at the foot of her bed

. . . that she hadn't eaten that biscuit.

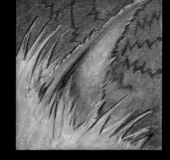

Deep in the night, Bridget awoke
when the moon was soon to rise.
She heard the sound of someone outside.
She smelled their scent as a wild dog can.

Into the light bounded Mrs Blair's dog calling,
"Time for some fun."

And
Bridget
went.

She romped in the gloom
with Mrs Blair's dog.

They tumbled in the shadows,
and the vegetable beds.

Then Mrs Blair's dog leapt
over the hedge.
Bridget went too . . .

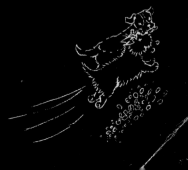

And was swept
on
the
night
wind
into the park,
into the dark,
to run and bark
with the rest of the
wild dog pack.

They promised a wolfish
Midnight Feast
to Bridget
and Mrs Blair's dog.
Then the wild hunt
sped up the hill . . .
past the bandstand,
the swings
and the paddling pool.

The moment the moon climbed to the sky,
the bandstand became a great meat pie

and heavenly sausages
rained from the stars.

Λnd when they all had eaten their fill

and Bridget was happy indeed that she'd eaten that biscuit . . .

UNTIL . . .

She thought of the baby,
her mum and her dad.
A dog for a daughter
might make them sad.
She gazed at the great
dog-biscuit moon,

and

HOWLED

so

LOUDLY

made

so much

DiN,

that the moon EXPLODED and the sky FELL IN.

Gone were the hounds.
Gone was the moon.
Bridget found herself back in her room
with a mum who had noticed
that something was wrong,
so at last . . .
Bridget told Mum about eating that biscuit.

"Mrs Blair was teasing," said Mum.

"She wasn't," sniffed Bridget. "Can't you see?"

"Not very well in the dark," smiled Mum,
"but you smell like my little girl to me.
Could we curl up like puppies,
just us two,
and tomorrow
we'll ask Mrs Blair what to do."

Bridget felt girlish again the next day
but they visited Mrs Blair anyway.

Mrs Blair shook her head.
"Of course it was a joke," she said.
"I'm sorry if I worried you.
Let's go in and brew some tea
and find my tin of human-being biscuits."

That did the trick.

And Mrs Blair's dog had one too.

Human-Being Biscuits!

Ingredients

125g butter

100g brown sugar

125ml golden syrup

1 egg yolk

350g plain flour

1 tablespoon ground ginger

1 teaspoon mixed spice

1 teaspoon bicarbonate of soda

Icing and sweets to decorate

Beat the butter and sugar in a bowl until it is pale and creamy.

Now whisk together the egg yolk and golden syrup. Add this goo
to the butter and sugar and mix well.

Stir in the flour, the bicarbonate of soda, the ginger and the spice.

Use your hands to squeeze the mixture. Squeeze it and pound it
until you have a smooth round lump of dough.

Next, let the dough have a rest. Cover it gently in a clingfilm sheet,
and pop it in the fridge for a thirty-minute sleep.

While you wait, grease your baking trays, preheat your oven to 180°C,
flour your work top then roll that dough. Roll until it's 4mm thick.
Now it's ready for your human-being-shaped cookie cutters.
(Avoid all bone-shaped cookie cutters. You never know what might happen.)

Place your human beings on the baking trays, spaced about 3cm apart,
and bake 'em up in the oven for 10 minutes, or until brown.

Remove them and allow them to cool. Then you can decorate with icing,
and maybe even human-being treats.

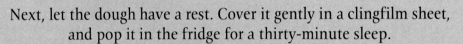

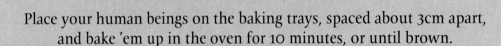

YOU MIGHT NEED HELP

FROM A GROWN-UP.